Night of the Veggie Monster

GEORGE McCLEMENTS

BLOOMSBURY

NEW YORK LONDON OXFORD NEW DELHI SYDNEY

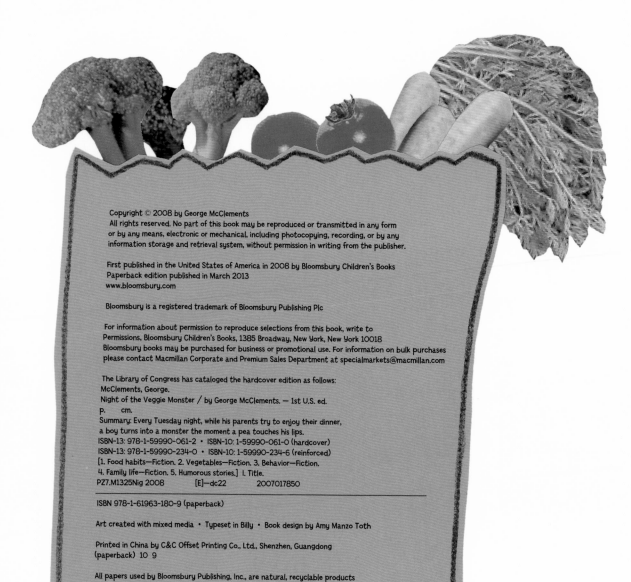

First published in the United States of America in 2008 by Bloomsbury Children's Books
Paperback edition published in March 2013
www.bloomsbury.com

Bloomsbury is a registered trademark of Bloomsbury Publishing Plc

For information about permission to reproduce selections from this book, write to
Permissions, Bloomsbury Children's Books, 1385 Broadway, New York, New York 10018
Bloomsbury books may be purchased for business or promotional use. For information on bulk purchases
please contact Macmillan Corporate and Premium Sales Department at specialmarkets@macmillan.com

The Library of Congress has cataloged the hardcover edition as follows:
McClements, George.
Night of the Veggie Monster / by George McClements. — 1st U.S. ed.
p.   cm.
Summary: Every Tuesday night, while his parents try to enjoy their dinner,
a boy turns into a monster the moment a pea touches his lips.
ISBN-13: 978-1-59990-061-2 • ISBN-10: 1-59990-061-0 (hardcover)
ISBN-13: 978-1-59990-234-0 • ISBN-10: 1-59990-234-6 (reinforced)
[1. Food habits—Fiction. 2. Vegetables—Fiction. 3. Behavior—Fiction.
4. Family life—Fiction. 5. Humorous stories.] I. Title.
PZ7.M1325Nig 2008   [E]—dc22   2007017850

ISBN 978-1-61963-180-9 (paperback)

Art created with mixed media • Typeset in Billy • Book design by Amy Manzo Toth

Printed in China by C&C Offset Printing Co., Ltd., Shenzhen, Guangdong
(paperback) 10 9

All papers used by Bloomsbury Publishing, Inc., are natural, recyclable products
made from wood grown in well-managed forests. The manufacturing processes
conform to the environmental regulations of the country of origin.

Green Is Good

Finicky Eaters

Vegetables 4 Kids

For my sweet peas:

Rachel, Samuel, and Matthew

Something **TERRIBLE** happens every Tuesday night.

It's not the **pork chops** or the **mashed potatoes**. It all starts when I'm forced to eat . . .

PEAS!

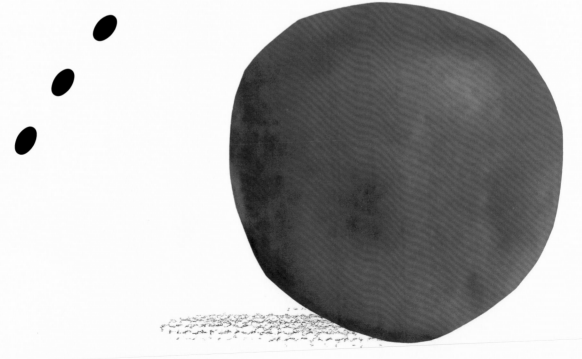

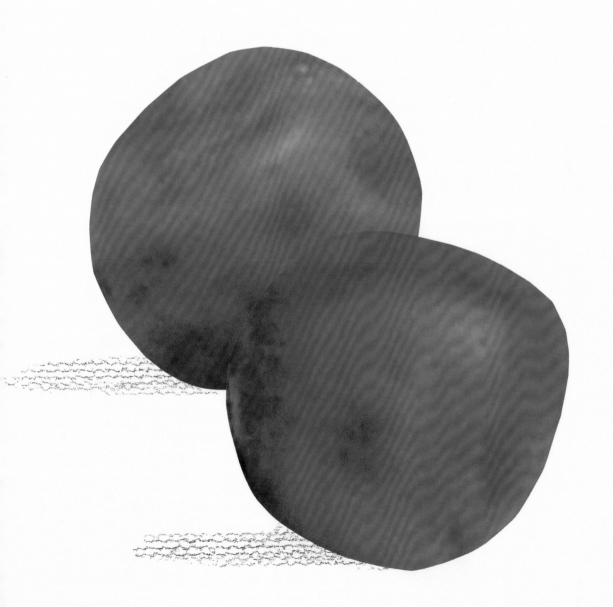

They have no idea what

one tiny pea

does to me.

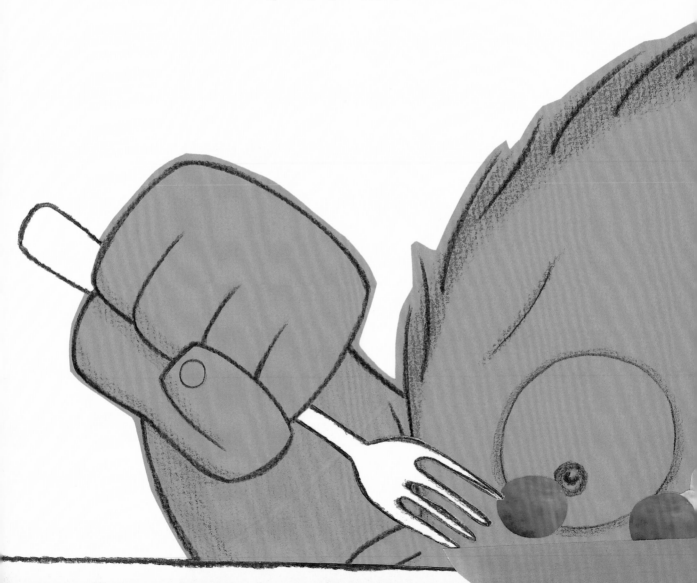

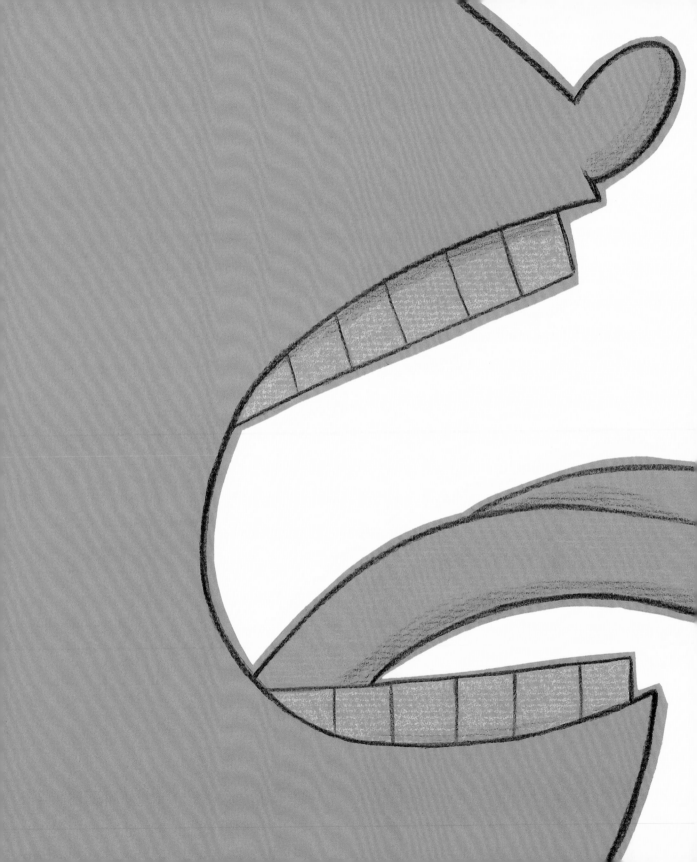

With just the

slightest

touch . . .

. . . it begins.

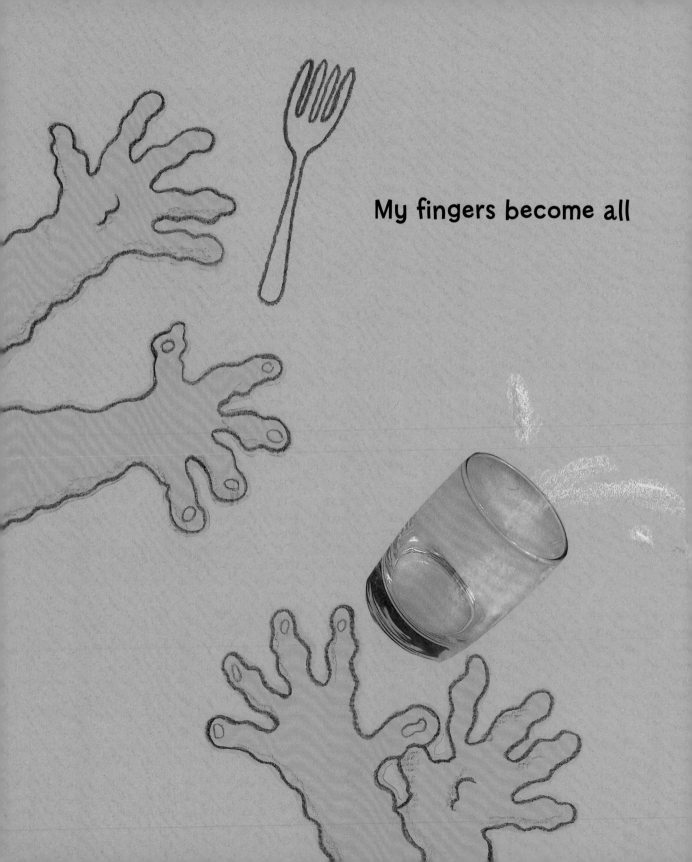

My fingers become all

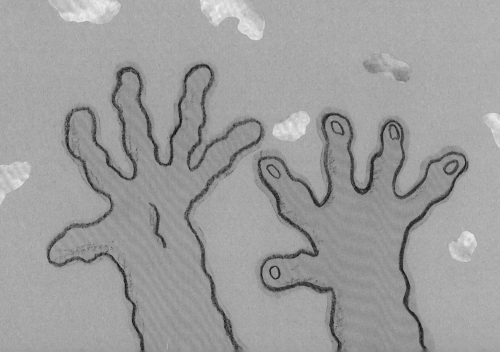

As the pea rests in my mouth,

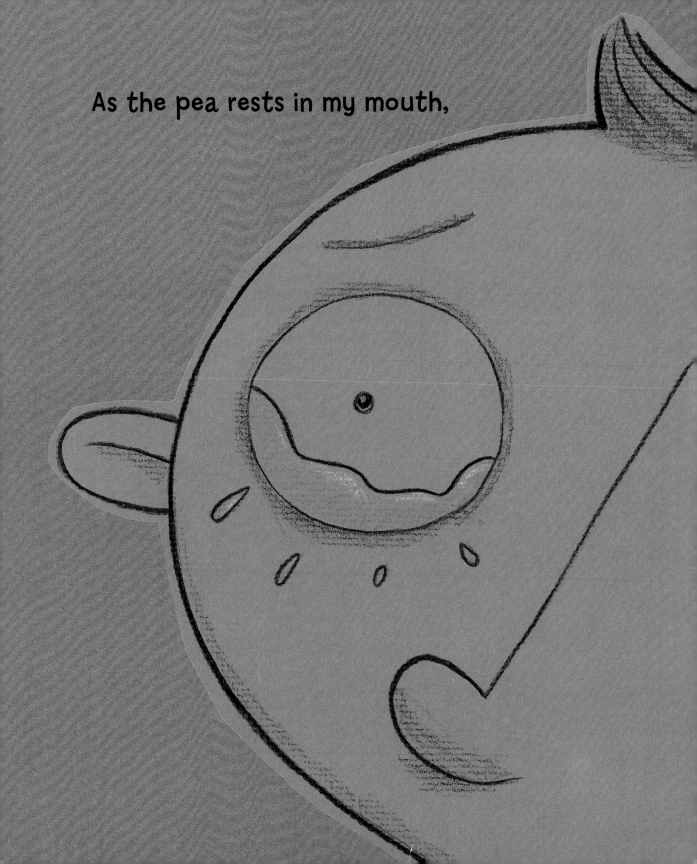

My toes
TWIST and
CURL UP
in my shoes.

I **SQUIRM** in my seat. I try to keep control but the **pea** is too strong. I start to transform into...

... a VEGGIE MONSTER!

Ready to **smash** the chairs!
Ready to *tip* the table!
Ready to...

. . . GULP!

I swallowed the pea.

I actually swallowed the pea.

It tasted all right, really.

Well, I guess peas are okay.
But there is still a danger!

Because **tomorrow** is WEDNESDAY, and on **WEDNESDAY** we have . . .